COULD HAVE BEEN FUNNY

GLYN WRIGHT

Could Have Been Funny

SP!KE

ISBN: 0 9518978 4 5

First published 1995 by
Spike
40 Canning Street
Liverpool L8 7NP

Spike acknowledges
the financial assistance of North West Arts Board.

Front cover photograph copyright the author.
Back cover photograph: Liverpool Echo.

Acknowledgements

Acknowledgements are due to the editors of the following publications in which some of these poems have appeared: Graffiti, Hybrid, The North, Norwich Writers' Circle Anthology 1994, Orbis, Rustic Rub, Smiths Knoll, Smoke, Tandem, Tears In The Fence and The Wide Skirt.

Others have been broadcast on BBC Radio Merseyside.

Contents

Snapped

I know I dreamed once I was a fan belt, gripping
my toes. And I knew if I snapped the thing would
grind and old Masters would blow a big gasket.
But I reckoned if I could just keep on going
Monday to Easter, Christmas to Friday, on and on.

I'm not sure when I started carrying old tights.
I had tights in my pocket and cupboard and desk:
all Annie's who left saying I was never at home.
I made it through Christmas and Easter and June
but didn't quite make the late summer close down.

We go to bed any time. Afternoons. I watch her head
moving up and down in sunlight, starlings on gutters.
I remembered that song. One time I climbed on stage:
And I will spin with Maggie till she falls asleep
and then I'll dance with Mary till the sun comes up.

The sky's never the same two days. And we seem to
manage. The wind on park lakes. I might just look
at shades of blue and say: Give us a touch, Jen.
And she does. So we go in, sliding up real slow.
And giggles. And underwear abandoned on stairs.

The Department Of Limbo

I chucked my sweatrag after the final bake,
packed my toolbox and oily bag:
tinsnips, mallets, gilbows, rule;
even shoved in my billycan and mug.

I couldn't believe when I passed the gate
that I wouldn't be back on Monday at seven,
but I'm queueing for a UB40, signing on.

This ain't the blissful nothing I dreamed
of doing those boxed-in afternoons of August,
more like waiting for your final judgement.

I'd rather wait on clock and hooter any day.
Give me back my overalls! Give us them now!
And let me sweat it out back there
in the floury inferno of the long red ovens.

On Your Dignity

Two days cleaning gutters, then nothing,
so down I goes to visit the old feller.
He's no longer sure who he is;
some days he thinks he's my uncle Jack
who got crushed by a crane on the docks.
Then I went to see about a roofing job
but the feller said no chance, his lad
just got his leg bit off by a loan shark.
I've got this dodgy toenail myself, bleeds
from too much tramping in rubby boots.

So I goes in the Bleak House for a swift half
and there's this academic at the bar;
he's got his haircut on back to front
and high turn-ups to show off his orange socks,
and he's spewing on about how in this country
the prophets are shut in dusty cupboards
and the people are really stupid,
and the newspapers are full of porno and hate
and the people are really really stupid.
He managed to get right up my nostril,
the left one mostly, but sometimes both.
He managed to get right down my welly,
wretching on about how the government was full
of nit-wits and gestapo and rank materialists
and the people were really really bloody stupid.

So I leaned across and said, "Excuse me. Pal.
But you're standing on my dignity there."
"Pardon?" he says, dead polite, turning to face me.
I said, a bit firmer, like, "You are standing
on my bloody dignity, pal."
"Oh, sorry," he says, taking a step back. "Sorry, mate."

Machines

They eat it up, grind it in steel cogs, iron jaws,
they crunch and masticate the silence,
spit out hard consonants of raw noise.

We who tend them grub for bits of quiet:
perched on a bench in the welding shop,
flicking ciggy ash in scurf and filings,

or outside by the scrapheap where wittery
sparrows dive to snatch at crumbs we drop
while we sit on metal drums at tea break.

If

I feed the machine. It eats boxes and my hours,
gobbles up days, years. I feed it empty cartons,
drop them on its endless rubber tongue.
It mutters while it feeds, shouts and grumbles.

I can't hear my own voice curse, my belly groan.
Once when I'd been out dancing late I'd turn over,
say: Stuff it. But now the big steel monster's boss
and it's never bored with munching, never weary.

It goes on like it's untouchable, immortal, but if
I leant that bit too far and bent its metal lip
so it caught in those grinding cast-iron teeth,
I could sit and watch it chew itself to pieces.

The Quiet Man

Marks a girth, scribes a pattern,
trims mild steel deftly as a tailor,
rolls each piece into an o
and grooves it at the throat.
His mallet regular as a pendulum
flanges each edge into tongue
or lips then glides one piece
into another as easily as p into i,
o into o to make tool or pipe.
Segment by segment
he shapes this lobster tail,
articulates the bend.

Where The Sexes Meet

The metal shop whiffs of grease, old handrags.
We arrive here dressed as ourselves and button up
uniform blue overalls to hammer, weld, strip down,
bash out conveyors that line the factory floor.

Foremen are brown coats. Managers swank
in spotless white, fierce with creases, prowl
the yards, the cubby holes to catch you out.
Think they're up to all the dodges.

Women are wrapped and knotted in white aprons,
packed in rows across the factory, seated
at belts that never stop while their overseer
scans them from a platform made by us.

The air's chocolate over there, butter, jam.
That's where the sexes meet when machines break down,
where you chat each other between ovens,
across conveyors, when backs are turned.

Bricklayers

Grouped up there
in the sun's kiln
they balance on planks.
Dry as socks,
tongues toss jibes
at office huts
while free hands flick
the thick grey muck
from pressed bricks.
One dusty clown
butters a brick-end
with mortar
like a boss
at a leisured breakfast.
A cloud of laughter
forms and falls.
And the sun bakes on
to stiffen and parch
the muck that bonds
these blocks of hard
compressed clay
that are set now
end to end.

Bricklayer

Before a numbing easterly
the collared man
lays bricks down the long wall
of a darkening afternoon.
His arm is automatic now
converting feint paper plans
into another man's house.
This is just another wall.
His trowel dabs muck
over each brick-end,
hand slaps the brick in place,
the ringing tool whips off
squashed muck, flicks it down
by his concreted boots.
Now he levels the line
with a trapped bubble,
taps a mayday
with the back of his trowel.
Now straightens, lumbago-backed,
as at a plank that might topple,
rubs with whitened hands
sucked dry by the mortar's leech.

Air

Down where no wind blows, no bird sings,
crouched in a tunnel of dark rock with shovel
and pick you hacked and hewed the earth's gut.

You whistled: I am master of any rock.
But its black dust bloomed on your skin,
flew past lips to snatch

your breath,
to squeeze
little by little

all
your air
out.

The Bushy

Mirrors make my muscles grow.
I got strong bunking in the big films.
We robbed a grey pipe from Froggy's yard,
made ace exterminators.
Dicko's dad give us a rusty saw.

We invaded the Bushy where daft kids mess:
Soft Jimmy with last year's diary, Gorpy Sue.
Dicko reckons they shag in there.
I've heard them saying love and stuff.
He says there's a fox and they talk to it.

They're well cracked. We phased them out
with skin-seeking shells. Dicko's dad told us
the daft-heads are bad for our blood
and once there was camps across the water.
Not like holiday places. Electric fences.

We wear sweatbands and piss on trains
and flattened some lad's watch on the rails.
Soft Jimmy says it's written in some book
he copied from that a great pest will
visit the earth and have to be vanquished.

All I've seen is hearts and scribble.
He believes it, though. He really does.
We fell about when he first said it.
Great pest? As if. I mean where would it
come from? And what would it look like?

Could Have Been Funny

They couldn't catch me at it, couldn't nail me.
They couldn't even get close to it,
I was too quick for them. Like I was charmed,
like I had a guardian angel. Maca had been
pulled loads of times. He was a loon.
He always had been a bit of a maddie,
but never as crazy as this: Penny Lane
he puts his foot down even harder.
We was in a two-litre injection job.
Race us? Maca had no chance, not
in that tin can he was in. He'd been
two miles behind all the way up the M6.
"You couldn't overtake a funeral,"
shouts Yozzer. We laughed.

But on Smithdown he does try and take us.
He's wide on the other side of the road
givin' us two fingers. Soon we was clockin'
seventy, but still he sticks out there
with Glocko and Wiggy and Jimbo givin' us the big grin.
"Let him think he's goin' past us," sez Yoz.
So I ease up a bit and let him get his bumper in front
and then I keep him there knowin' I've got plenty
in reserve. An' just as he thinks he's gonna take us
I hit the pedal, give it loads.
But I only edge in front. An' Maca stays
out there on the wrong side of the road
with a motor comin' the other way.
An' just stays there. An' stays there. An' stays there.

Our car goes quiet now. We're watchin' them
go towards each other. He was tryin'
to make me back off and let him in
and I was waitin' for him to drop off.
But he didn't. He just keeps on goin'.
The other car was flashin' him to get in,
they was nearly on top of each other.
I stamps the brake down. Maca tries
to swerve in. The other car skids.
I seen Maca come out through the windscreen.
He was kind of flyin'.
He comes down in the middle of the road.
Jeez, it was horrible, too horrible to look at,
got straight to your guts.

I jumps out, dashes to this alehouse,
grabs the phone, does treble nine:
"Ambulances, need ambulances. There's been a smash."
"What's your number please?" the voice is sayin'.
I sez, "Never mind me number. There's people
lyin' all over the road out there!"
"What's your number, please?" the voice sez, dead calm.
I give her the number and went back outside,
and seen fellers standin' out there watchin'.
Seen people helpin' the driver out of the motor
that Maca had hit. Seen Glocko
with blood soakin' into his shirt.
He was mumblin' and cryin'.
Not words, just noises like a baby.

Maca hadn't moved. He was in a heap
with people crowdin' round him, bendin' over.
Seen Wiggy leanin' against the cemetery wall.
Seen Jimbo sat in the road with his head in his arms,
seen him stand and stagger like he's sunk ten pints,
seen his legs go from underneath him,
seen him fold up on the oil and broken glass.
So I legged across to pick him up.
"Oh, you mustn't move him," sez this old feller in a cap,
"you must leave him where he is till the medics come."
I sez, "Will you piss off yer old fossil."
He sez, "I've been in the St John's Ambulance - "
I sez, "I don't care where you've been
this is my mate lyin' here in all this shite!"

So I picked Jimbo up, but he started groanin'
so I put him down just out of the oil and glass.
An' then I seen loads of people all around,
and all their voices was mixed together:
What happened? How could it? Whose fault?
This one comin' that way. That one comin' this way.
Wrong side. Terrible. Oh God. Oh Jeez. Oh Hell.
An' then I hears Wiggy start ramblin',
"I'll make a statement, just giz a solicitor,
I'll sign a confession, just giz a pen."
An' there's no one near him, just a dog with three legs.
An' then I seen a woman put a blanket over Maca's head,
and his feet was stickin' out the other end
like he's gone to bed with his trainees on.

An' then I hear them: Ner-ner-ner-ner.
An' Yozzer starts yellin' at me, "Come 'head, Robbo.
Move it. Give it legs, the Force is comin'!"
An' Wiggy's tellin' the dog he'll make a statement.
An' the dog's lookin' at him like he's cracked.
Ner-ner-ner-ner-ner-ner.
An' Yozzer's screamin' down me ear, "Robbo!
Will you shift yer arse, the Force is here.
They'll have you. You'll go down if they grip you!"
An' Wiggy.
An' Yozzer.
An' the dog.
An' Maca.
An' me legs won't move.

Ner-ner.
Ner.
Ner.
An' Wiggy's confessin' to a three legged dog.
An' Maca's in bed with his trainees on.
An' me legs won't move.
So I'll get sent down.
Ner-ner.
Ro-bbo.
Ner-ner.
Come and get me.
Ner-ner ner...
It could have been dead funny
but Jeez it weren't.

Snarling Tool

They call me Baldy, Old Git. Reckon it only
takes two years to learn what took us five.
Indentured, I was: apprentice sheet metal worker.
Half what we know is useless. So they say.
One lad reckons he'll be doing something else
by the time he's thirty-five. We built up
tool kits to last a lifetime: old tradesmen
gave you hammers, mallets, to start you off.

I made a copper kettle once, won a prize.
I worked the sheet up on a block of oak,
the base was a perfect disc wired on a jenny.
My mother said the spout was like
a swan's neck with an open beak.
That was the tricky part: to shape the curve;
I had to use a mallet of rolled hide,
work it on a funnel stake and treblet.

These lads don't know half the stakes
never mind the tongs and rivets.
They call them: This one; or: That one there.
First thing I did was learn the names.
Feller said to me: "Names was made to be spoke
and if they're not they die, so learn them."
So I did: bick iron, half moon stake,
sugar loaf mandel, swage block, horse.

Old blacksmiths, tinkers, left us those names:
creasing iron, hatchet stake, anvil horns.
All this lot know is flashy motors, fancy drinks:
Coca Cola, Ford Capri. They could name you
every maxi burger in the High Street,
could read the label on a stripy shirt
from a hundred yards in a dreadful light
but they wouldn't know a ball head from a snarling tool.

24

Restless

I've always liked cats: the way they live out
in the night, and walls are no object. Anyway.
It only happened once. I was surprised myself.
But I'd been feeling kind-of restless for a while.
It was a typical summer coach trip:
luggage racks full of ale and all hands
pairing off on the way back. I finished up
snogging with Lil from the print shop.
I didn't know she was like that,
she never lets anyone touch her machine.

When the driver dropped us on the corner
we slipped down this alley and carried on,
and slap led to tickle and that led to squeeze
and before I knew it I was stood there
with my pants round my ankles committing
adultery, fornicating in a public place
with Dolly Baker's mog watching from a backyard wall.

Never happened again. Just the once.
I'd been brought up going to chapel twice a week.
Next time I felt that restless thing come on
I took up fishing. Once I caught a monster pike.
It was nice, though, that time with Lil.
I know I shouldn't say this, but at my age...
You could feel the night breeze on your arse,
and we just seemed to fit together real neat.
And the cat must have enjoyed it, too:
it had nine kittens that year.

Wisecrack

I am wisecrack. I am laugh-a-minute.
I am the one who is never lost for words;
keeping one-liners like dog-ends behind my ear,
I roll along the pavement's heaving deck:
stiff back, big shoulder, tight arse.

I bend my elbow for halves of bitter,
jab my finger at posers and bossmen,
twist my lip at busybody coppers.
I say: These dockers are the best in the world.
I say: My people are the salt of the earth.

I say: Remember the days down in old Scotty Road
when no-one locked their door, the days
before our city had its heart ripped out.
This damned pain hooks around my breastbone now,
my chest blows like a dud concertina.

And it's no music to sing to, let alone dance.
You name a dust and I have shovelled it
down in the hold: rice bran, asbestos, coal...
All mirrors call me paleface now,
or worse. The cruellest call me shadow.

Tell me I'm living in a dead man's skin.
But then I lean close and laugh at the glass
and say: I've had some great sessions
in The Blue House, The Goat, and The Legs Of Man.
I've seen the Blues bring home the cup. Twice.

And once I bred a champion pigeon.
Yes, I've elbowed my brother out of the road
to get in the gang when a good ship come in
but I was no man's handrag or doormat or stooge
in all them years on the windy wharf.

When I shifted salt and coal and tobacco and flour
and cotton and timber and iron pyrites,
when I had the shite of the world on my sleeve.
I say this to the glass
and my hot words leave a fog on my face.

Bessie McGrath On The Docks

We was working down the dreaded Baggie;
had to shake out used bags and sacks,
stitch them in a bundle two foot thick
then throw them up and stack them high.
And the muck in that place: there was that much dust
and filth and fibres in the air, you had to part it
like a curtain just to glimpse each other.
You didn't blow your nose, you called the chimney sweep.

Then we heard they was starting people on the docks
so we all traipsed down there. And got took on.
Five bob a day it was, double what the Baggie paid,
for shifting cotton bales from quay to warehouse.
But men would nudge each other and snatch
the fag-ends from mouths that turned to fog-horns,
and when we raised our noses to their skits
they started muscling at the management.

They said the work was too hard for "tarts", too mucky,
and they felt awkward having to watch their language
while they grafted, so we'd have to go, or else.
The salt of the earth, they call themselves,
well I can think of other names that fit.
After three months of being leaned on very heavy
the company give in. We got the sack
and went back down the Baggie, and felt the pinch.

The Mary Ellens

They called us the Mary Ellens of the boats,
up and down gangplank with buckets of cold water,
soaping and scrubbing and swilling off; polishing
brasswork till your face looked back we sang:
Vicar oh vicar please stuff your revelations...

Those sea winds whipped our faces raw. Winter nights
your handrag froze. This scouring stuff like gritty acid
near took off skin as we balanced on trestles, sang:
Vicar oh vicar please stuff your revelations
just give us a feller with a dick like a donkey.

We paraded like an aproned army when job was done.
Starched and spotless. Our boss marched decks
like a bowler-hatted general going cross-eyed
staring at his tips, while we whispered at his back:
Fingers like parsnips and a dick like a radish.

I had the cleanest step in our street, but you
couldn't escape dirt: coaldust and carbon black.
You scrubbed your house but bugs hid in the wall.
Only in church, you shut the door on muck and sang:
There is a green hill far away; Jerusalem the Golden.

Seeing The World

I was between ports all my life, in fo'c'sles
that reeked of paint and socks and stale tobacco,
scoffing mushy peas and stale plum duff.
But a week on land did me, seven nights of shindigs
and I'd get that old urge to glimpse the albatross.
I've stared up Mount Fuji and down Vesuvius,
sailed the doldrums and hurricane and fog five days thick,
seen shark fins in the eye of the storm,
witnessed the glory of the Great White Whale
and I've fed on crusts and water in a Lisbon cell,
and when I was sixteen in Buenos Aires a woman
called me Blondie and touched the buckle on my belt.

The days drift by me now like distant birds
and all the ports that I have docked in
seem like names that could be anywhere or nowhere.
They might be places some other deckie berthed in
and bragged of through an epic session
leaning on a bar down Paradise Street.
I collar people in the pub. I name the names:
Freemantle, Cape Town, Trincomalee
and then I'm almost there if I've supped enough.
But folk must think me a daft old bugger,
this face like paper, all screwed up and yellow,
surrounded by a toilet brush of bristles.

I have aches to remind me where my joints are;
I rub on hot ointment but they come gnawing back.
Soon I won't know pain or regret or the taste of ale.
So many I shipped out with have gone that way already:
Vaughan, McTaggart, Ryan, Morrissey,
Jones who played the concertina, Jackson who had
the clap so many times they called him Big Hand.
I held McTaggart's ashes in his pewter mug
and tipped them from the pier. I sailed with him
more than thirty years. He's just a name now
whispered across a table full of pint pots
by old men waiting to go the way he went.

But I did what I set out to do. At least, I saw
a lot of sea and all the bars around the edge
and no-one and nothing ever tied me down.
So I've had to make all my own arrangements.
They won't bury me in no damp earth like Ryan
and McMahon. I want to go like Squeezebox Jones
in a sheet weighed down with lumps of iron
to sink through fathoms and feed the fish that feed
the dolphin and the whale and the black-browed albatross;
but like McTaggart and Vaughan and Banjo Bull
I'll go back to sea as a film of ash
and let the ebbtide carry me where it will.

Wildcat Shadows

I'd have been a damn fine mother, always hankering.
So now I'm Old Dear in the end house no-one knocks at,
Mumbler mocked by street-kids chattering stardom.
I don't trouble Postie much. My mantelpiece is crammed
with scraps: boomerang and bongos, bits of carved driftwood,
my old man's histories: Blue Funnel and White Star.

I told him when he raged: Yes, I would like sons, but
I won't be lumbered with a feller, with needles and socks
and pans of cabbage. I want to sail the world like you.
Regret, he said. You see. Only a slip. Don't know your own.
A woman's place. Natural. Shuttup and listen. What you're
told. Little madam. Raise your voice to me. I'll take my belt.

You were just a servant on the boat, practising
being invisible, palming creases, chasing dust,
only appearing at snap of fingers, ding of bell.
Most toffs were just big babies when the sea
turned wild, they'd grab your sleeves, your skirts,
fall crying in your arms begging you not to go.

Still, my father nags. He's in the walls, the chairbacks.
But I tell him: Scented islands. Tasman Sea. Port of Spain
and Adelaide. I lay out beneath the Southern Cross,
Andromeda and Aquarius, saw Jupiter through a jungle roof,
saw iron steps ripped off by waves, and zigzag shark fins
and humming birds and wildcat shadows in the night.

I throw all this at him until his nagging stops, tell him,
tell him, tell him till his infernal tongue wraps up.

Ledge Life

I sit at this ledge crammed with flower pots,
gaze across street, old docks, grey river,
watch the sound ships of my youth throb past,
cry dislocated shanties through flaking lips:
Haul away boys, away; Lift the big blue anchor;
We're bound next tide for Africa.

Once I'd carve the bones of shark and whale.
Buttons mock my fingers now, like doorway kids.

Once I rode an elephant, shouldered orange monkeys.
I shared Big Lilla's blanket, did things
would make my good wife dizzy. Like sucking
melon, supping stout, honey from the comb.

Blessed Alice would rather polish chapel pews,
mouth hymn and psalm, lick charity envelopes.

My plants are only inches yet, green paper
scraps on shiny pencils, but soon they'll swell,
reach for light, scramble for the curtain rail.
I'll not see out. They'll blank the empty quay
and boatless water with a forest of leaf and stem
and scarlet fruit as big as an elephant's balls.

Mungo Park's Journey Of Discovery

Squinted at the spotlight of the Gambian sun
and made himself deaf to promptings of delay,
led off his stringy column through a land
of gloom that held hot fingers to the windpipe.

Nights, while croaking pits distracted them,
the villain darkness slit unguarded bundles,
scooped handfuls of amber, trinkets, gold.
Tornadoes entered with flourishes, tossed away hats.

Fierce drumming announced the rainy season;
pantomime asses danced on rocky ledges, flipped.
Soldiers hammed at slack-paced drunks, lay down
in pools and closed their eyes to the rain's soft story.

Sick men were stored in grass-rooofed huts
but Sergeant McGee, Privates Hill and Purvey
were written out between Toniba and Bambikoo,
and Lawrence Cahill was dragged into a far
different horror when a lurking wolfpack pounced.

At Sandsanding, scenes of love and death:
Park boiled strong decoctions of cinchona, nursed
the fevered Anderson on a bed of bullockhides.

Watching the life drip from his closest friend
he turned to Allie back at home. "I long
very much to be with you, my love," he told her
across immensities of bush and ocean.

From a kit of old canoes he built a patchwork boat,
launched it as HMS Joliba and set out
to shoot a hole through any tribes
that barred its way to rivermouth and sea.

All warrior-craft were blasted from the river
whose banks pulsated with spear and shield
until an army of a thousand bowmen massed
around a single doorway in the rocks.

Here the big battle scene was set:
lone whites crumpled by hissing arrows,
tribesmen toppling by the rank
before the bronchial cough of muskets.

When raging waters juggled with their vessel
frightened soldiers offered sabres, trinkets,
grains of amber, sextant, gold, and
bolts of cotton wrapped in hides of antelope.

Dodging arrows, his boat a tossed banana,
the tragic Mungo spoke for one last time
to his beloved Allie, and when the script ran out
took Abraham Bolton in his arms.

Lieutenant Martyn paired off with the unclaimed private
and at Park's nodded signal for the final exit
both couples waltzed into the angry river
whose rapids took them like a broken trinket.

The House Of Rayon

You talked dirty money in the counting house,
lashing up deals, plotting to fix and clinch,
then going out to higgle, hawk and chaff:
callico, rayon, worsted, crepe.

This meet, I had the rough lines ready:
You don't like it when the heat is up,
go sit in the fridge; you don't want to play
my numbers, I blow you off the gamefield.

But when it came, I couldn't produce.
I talked two hours about my old man,
left my phone someplace, my timepiece,
half my clothes in another room.

I was white satin being drawn
and drawn again, oh so slowly
across dark velvet; I was left
spread out, uncreased, immaculate.

Beyond Sand And Feather

Before I had you I paced each day this gusty shore
where waders pipe the seasons in and out, gazing
vigilant for flashes above the sea's torn silk.

Out beyond sand and feather, the bones of winter dead,
a bell-buoy swings its hammer. And I am left with
two's of things, with snapshots and half-used perfume.

*   *   *

The streets wait for night; today is almost history,
not quite silence. The cool sky is purple
and pierced now by the stars of Aquila, the Eagle.

Lights blink out, cats drop from back walls
and I shape stories from scraps, recount my days
to you, but only stacked terraces murmur back.

*   *   *

And wild geese will trumpet the long Arctic flight
and warblers will straggle back from Africa
and there will be days of sudden iridescence.

And I shall be scattered at the roots of oak
and all who spoke your name will be gone
like the swifts that whistled round your rooftop.

*   *   *

I dig around passionflower, phlox and lily,
scatter handfuls of crushed bark, humus, leafmould;
turn over the bare soil between apple and pear.

I tell myself, love, that I am doing this for you
but that ragged old crow rocks glossy-backed
on the chimney pot and tells me: Nah, nah, nah!

Knowing Plenty

I bought the dish with my pay-off, got the biggest
the roof would hold. There's a lot of domes in Kabul
and different militias. And the tribesmen in New Guinea
wear penis sheaths and rub mud on their bodies,
and the ones in Brazil blow crazy powder up each other's noses,
but if the factions in the eastern suburbs join
with the ones in the south, the Afghan government's
going to have real problems. There's an update due
any minute. But even when shells are falling
you see men carrying cans of water on poles.
And when the Amazon floods it carries away palm trees
and farmers' shacks and dead pigs. And if you stand
in the river having a wee then a tiny fish
will swim deep into your willy and live there,
so don't say I didn't warn you.
Things happen so quickly. I came down from bathroom
and saw three Afrikaners lying dead in the road.
I went out to let the missus in and diamonds had fallen
two points on Wall Street. You can't afford to be out
for a second. I keep telling her to take her key.
She sits in the kitchen with her head in her arms.
I don't know what's wrong with the woman.
She hasn't been the same since the president
of the World Bank resigned. Or was he sacked? No, that
was the French Foreign Minister over the mess in Africa.
Burundi is about to cut itself to shreds
and the prospects in Guinea are worse than hell,
and the missus keeps wanting to talk about the hole
in the roof where the dish is attached, but I tell her:
As long as you remember to empty the bucket, what's
all the fuss about? And she wants to go to the park.

Park? I said. Park? You've got an equatorial rainforest
coming up after the commercial break, there's a group
of soldiers lost out there. My life. I don't know. Some people.
Then the social called me in, asked what I'd been doing
to find work. Work? I said. Work? The tin miners
in Bolivia have been on strike for a month
and the Chinese silkworm trade has almost collapsed.
He said: But Mr Smith. I said: Don't you try and tell me
about work, one in three Sicilian olive-pickers
has been reduced to begging and the mountain tribes
of Thailand have been forced to grow cabbages. Some people.
Like my missus, she invites her relations round
and they sit here talking. Talking. No interest at all
in the Tokyo banking scandal. She says they don't
understand Japanese. But they never will if they don't
make the effort. I'm learning Croatian from a tape.
I have trouble with their weather forecasters.
They talk so fast, especially when there's shelling
around the T.V. station. It's been raining since dawn
in Trinidad, and they're expecting a heavy frost
in the eastern parts of Transylvania above a thousand feet.
Oh, and the Mexican president has just been assassinated.
The world's so small nowadays. We know so much.
It's incredible.

The Bit Part Players

1

We could hear the news chimes ringing
as we moved on deeper in
watched by a wild cat's polished skull
and a carved mahogany hawk.
An oak desk stood upended
on a crystal chandelier,
and a headless statue guarded
a house without a door.
Then a darting fox went ducking
through a fence of iron spears
as this figure in a baseball cap
came lumbering through the gloom.

"I fired men for coughing wrong. My slaves
smashed out nuggets and syphoned black juice.
I bathed in bubbly, gorged on bullmeat.
I bought posh pussycats and medicine men,
snapped up newspapers, governments, empires.
My rivals caballed: armadas of figure-hacks
blasted my flagship and my brain combusted;
a blazing forest of parrot screams,
elephant thunder and dusty palpitations,
vipers uncurling from my eardrum.
It shrivelled the bollocks of my pursemen,
greyhats battered me with legal gibberish,
stripped me by method, mountain by seabed,
seized my marble bath, my Silver Cloud.
I collared scribblers, offered sole rights
on The Man Who Turned It All To Crap.
They did headshakes, saying: We know that one,
it's been done too many times before."

2

The column sighed through a chill mist,
the sighing column straggled through
this place of broken bricks;
blank eyes down or lost far off,
hooded men and headscarved women
wandered quite oblivious through
this place of long-dead trees,
save for one who stopped and turned.

"The grey rising paths broke up as we climbed
away from white houses and flat yellow fields
grandfathers and great aunts had won from black bog;
a land where we grew, scaring songbird and rook
from sunflower and maize, gripping handle and rein
as we chanted old songs to the fresh-seeded furrow.
They roared in with rifles as we shouldered baled hay,
screamed as from that day we no longer lived there,
they were clearing their land of our long bony faces.
We could name all those men, they had sipped our peach wine,
and fingered their fiddles when we lifted our flutes.
Now stone buzzards eyed us from high sheer ledges
as we headed for white peaks the old ones came over
snatching up root-scraps, dry twigs and bark
from crumbled grey slopes where little would grow
but couch grass and tyme and stunted wee oak
and bitter old songs young voices made new."

3

As the drinkers circled a low yellow fire
clapping hands at flames and sizzling wood,
this thin man in a torn blue suit
stepped out of the smoke.

"She didn't even know how to dress
never mind conduct an interview:
blue trousers and some stupid hat,
I'd seen smarter refugees.
They called me Master of the Verbal Ambush.
If a question needed to be asked I was the man.
I was nosy, persistent and unflappable
and no politician could intimidate me.
I got behind the mask to expose
selfservers and shameless liars.
I'd let them ramble till I spotted a crack.
Halfway through she took out this folder.
Once I'd been treasurer of the Guild.
There was always gossip about dodgy figures
but no-one ever produced solid numbers.
When she started throwing filth
I refused to take any more questions.
I said: If you'll excuse me now, I have
to go down to the make-up room."

4

As a jukebox minstrel whined for home
and a grunting engine faltered,
this alley fox went nosing
through the binbags and the trash,
then away past padlocked iron gates
and gutted pavement lights
where a man stood with a suitcase
looking very lost.

"The old ones said I would grow to be a storyteller.
I had no feel for dusty soil, dour routines
of vineyard and olive grove. Always
I preferred the tales of women, the songs
of old men to fields where only the wind speaks;
always riddles and proverbs, chants and ballads,
lines and phrases from the holy book. Now
I move between capitals, my best suit in a folded bag,
tell how water has been stolen from our rivers,
the leaves from our trees, how canisters fall
from clear skies like a million cans of lemonade.
Days, I haunt embassies and studios saying:
We cannot defeat the iron general alone
but maybe with help, and then perhaps one day
we will be called on by you or some other.
Nights, I sit with holy book and riddles
reading what I already know by heart: And we will
surely meet once more, after just another sunrise
or perhaps a hundred I will surely see you
where the roads cross, I will surely meet you there.
Some nights I ask lampshades and the walls:
Have my people for a thousand years
been speaking to the wind?"

5

Down beside this moonlit pool
a soldier knelt and dipped his hands;
as a dogfox barked through the darkness
he plunged those hands in deeper,
then pulling back from broken water
spoke slowly to his dripping fingers.

"My mother told me: No Cissy, big boys don't cry.
My father said: Put your fists up Champ.
As I sat by the window the girl walked from the store;
I didn't think or decide, just moved to the door.
The officer said: Agincourt, Crecy and Trafalgar,
we cut them to pieces and that's a proud tradition.
The sergeant said: This is a rifle and this is a bullet
and they are more important to you than anything.
The corporal said: There's no such thing as pain.
And in the mess the lads would shout: Pussy-pussy-pussy,
bam-bam-bam; we are the champions of the world.
I stayed well behind, but kept her in sight,
my feet going silent like I'd been taught,
till she turned down an alley past the last street light."

6

Beyond the long and rusted fence,
in there with heaps of dry leaves
and tall grey poppy heads,
in there with twisted droppings
of the wandering urban fox,
a man with a spade bent his body,
turned over the damp dark earth.

"I came back; it's been a long time. Years.
My old man had a plot here. Down there
they said: We will write your name in lights
big and bright, high up there flashing;
then told me my face wasn't shaped
quite right, jaws were going out of fashion.
I've learned a lot: How to sip cheap wine
and grin with one hand in my trouser pocket.
A woman stopped me at the stage door once, said:
I will lick you till you cannot bear it.
But I'd get sick before a telly interview.
It didn't seem like a hard decision,
just like once I knew I had to get away,
not to live the way my old man had.
Pity he's not alive. I could have asked him.
There's a black-headed bird, sings in brambles.
I'd like to know its name."

7

Through this place of fallen headstones
a dogfox darted through the birches
watched by a woman from the stump of a tree.

"They take me back and tut. But I'll go again.
All days taste of disinfectant there; grey ceilings flake.
We have tea at four and folk who forget their names
sniff at Jack who talks of all the women he's kissed.
If only he could manage more than that, I say,
and some almost choke on their egg and cress.
My children tell me off, call me naughty mum.
I'm Busy Lizzie. Always. On Dad's farm: pigsty
and henhouses where swallows came each May
to nest in cups of mud. Wild geese and blackcap warblers.
And harriers floating in just above the earth.
My Billy would have understood.
I cleaned big cargo boats and ocean liners,
out all weathers, then dances over Lacey's pawnshop.
And such skies above the river, like sparkling blue,
clouds of lace and forktailed birds that dived.
After breakfast you shuffle to the telly room.
And finish needing to be bathed. I birthed five:
fed and shod and scrubbed them. And scolded, too: That Billy,
scallywag running with untied laces. And I knew
that day I heard the roar of his first motorbike.
But he's the one would have understood.
I watched this film: some place with roofs of grass,
an old woman and her son, he carried her on his back
through stony hills, up gentle bushy slopes,
eased her down in a valley, kissed her, and when he'd gone
she lay and watched the changing sky, cloud and moon, listened
for this bird, a melody for those passing out of life."

8

As she moved away through the twilight
past a tumbled obelisk
and fallen granite crosses,
an owl sailed in on rounded wings
and a vixen joined the dogfox
in the birches on the edge.

Resist, said the moss on a blackened stone.
Resist, said the stone and the owl gave a hoot
as the dogfox climbed on the vixen's back
to make a single fearless beast
that thrusted at the spreading dark.

As the light died in the graveyard
we gathered up the broken stones,
the wet and grassy white rock,
found for it a new shape:
a disc of shattered marble
on a mossy fallen slab.

As the foxes watched from the birches
we set beside the marble disc:
redbrick fragments, woodash, pebbles,
polished skull of a big wild cat,
round grey heads of poppy seeds,
spotless feather from the wing of a swan
and a carved mahogany hawk.

Resist, said the stone in the dying light
as the foxes faded through the birches
and the owl perched in a pine tree
going hoo-hoo-hooh!

As the darkness closed the pale disc tried
to cling to what remained of light;
but that owl stayed in the pine tree
going hoo-hoo-hooh!

Caller

A celebrant, he calls with bucket
and cloth, shouldered ladder. Of all
workmen he has the cleanest
hands; his arms are dark,
inscribed with purple symbols.
Seeing knives and serpents
one might suspect the devil
yet his fingers are pink as any priest.

Ceremonious, he dips
wrist-deep through steam, strangles
the sacrificial, dripping cloth and yields
of it a scourge to practise
flagellation on the air, then flays
his back in just a single stroke
of divine punishment. For example
he wears the whip on his shoulder
as he ascends, lightly laying on his hands.

Raised up, he ministers
stiff at first, along fixed lines
then loosening into curves,
flourishes, rapid scribed circles;
a dazzling argument of handplay.
Thus he works, purifying our vision,
offering an illuminated world
through cleansed glass.

Only after he has collected
his coins and gone do we see
the dirt left in angles,
along edges, the smudged strokes
of his imperfect hand.

History Man

"In nineteen hundred and...*Oh My God*...
Chamberlain's plans to build a sewage system..."
Bumstead has just prowled past with a list
of staff who cannot cope. I may be pencilled in.
Last lesson was a riot: two chairs broken,
duster out the window. This lot are
mercifully quiet, if much too close to sleep.
Jenny Ball is confessing her love for ANARCHY
to her desktop - ah, such a spicy girl, and sharp:
she says I could do useful work with insomniacs.

Ah, so long ago that I wanted to be Leon Trotsky,
dashing to exile in two fur coats,
gold coins sewn into the heels of my boots;
commanding an insurgent army from a train;
laying with Natalia my devoted revolutionary concubine.
It might have been me who wrote that history
is slow, barbarously slow, implacably cruel,
yet it goes on, and we believe in it.

But now that I am deep into old fart territory
I'd settle for being Caligula;
to bathe in spikenard and oil of violet,
and select Jenny Ball as my latest bride
while Bully Bumstead falls on his knees as I pass.
I'd mount the great white horse, go clip-clopping down
the reeky corridors, canter through the rusty gates
away from Chamberlain and his sewers, from duty lists
and termly tests and kids who left hankies
and workbooks and manners at home,
away past burned-out motors and mean barbarian
estates and on to circuses and to Rome.

The Follower

A youthful convert of the tainted streets,
I pursued my paragon, the stern apostle,
through unquiet multitudes as he
held out before me a kingless domain,
a fenceless territory of peace.

His grave orations were a curse
falling on the avenues of privilege,
his upraised fist a knuckly thundercloud
set to crack above the heads
of the intolerant and the wicked.

He promised fire like a million serpents
unwinding over a trembling earth,
offered the leafy zones of dream
forested from the seeds of flame.

In mute respect I inclined my head;
he lifted raw thoughts to his palm,
worked them between persuasive fingers,
moulding each exactly to his own.
I walked out speaking those words he'd handed,
coloured my phrases with his images.

Till my jaw wearied of hard-covered concepts
and I noticed the comic hairs in his upturned nose.

One weird day I untopped my pen
as strange ideas whirred behind my eyes;
unruly ink rioted from the nib:
bursting from tight margins it surged
down gaps between his august lines.

My hero's critical eyebrows soared,
thin lips struggled with *snake* and *turncoat*
as his jerking shoulder huffed away.

Key axioms
and precepts
lay between
my footprints
as I scattered
his collected speeches,
marked my path
away from his
with essential
but abandoned
texts.

The Rope Thrower

They gripped my hand, called me the Rope Thrower.
I could drop a loop on the neck of a stallion
at full gallop. I'd lived with a woman up there.
We used to make it in the high grass
between fruit trees, bare arses to the moon.

"Wolves that run through the mountains,"
he called them, ordered me to attack.
I resigned. But then I wasn't so sure.
I wasn't a rough mountain man any more,
I washed in a patterned bowl, owned a book,
had a proper wife with shoes and hats.
And there were hillsides of virgin land to be had.
And he was a big man, bigger than a grizzly
and twice as fierce; sharp as a desert cactus;
a tongue on him smooth as a preacher,
he called the land a princely realm,
said it was our destiny to seize it.

I started to bring in their herds, darkened
the sky with burning corn. But it wasn't enough.
Nowhere near. I had to kill or capture all the men.
He even wrote down what I had to say; "We will not
make peace until you cease to move."
They had shrunk to men of bone and rags,
blanket-covered mounds between the rocks.
"Too much snow," I stalled. "Not enough mules."
"Invade,". he spat. "Now! No delay. Invade!"

We stumbled through high passes knee deep in snow,
closed on them like a pair of claws.
They stood on ledges tossing stones, hurled
branches, roots and curse after goddam curse.
"You have a day to surrender," I told them.
Then I had all the orchards hacked down.

The canyon was filled with the sound of axes
as the peach trees cracked and toppled:
five thousand ancient trees. That broke their spirit,
it snapped like wood under the blade.
They started to come in. Lines of dead men, mute
and blind, passed me like I wasn't there. Choked me, that.
Not a word. Not then, or ever. Not snake-tongue
or coyote. Not scorpion or skunk. Not even the Lynch Man.

As Close To Heaven As We'll Ever Be

Up here, I think of you when my brain thaws:
your mauve lips poised to receive flute,
your painted finger crooked over the long pipe.
Our captain says we must not give away locations -
as if we have a clue - and remain always vigilant.
We do much splashing up rock paths chanting filth
in case a band of deluded redhats should charge
believing they would rather squat here in our place.
We're told to keep our pecker up and think of
loved ones and regiment and a mission that has
taken us as close to heaven as we'll ever be.

I've practised growing wings but managed only rashes.
When the sky comes down we see nothing for weeks,
in summer there is just one hailstorm a day, though
the ice makes passable tea if you can find a twig.
But the stone teeth of the slopes eat our boots
and your book grew a fur coat down in the forest
so I will return an expert on chilblains and mould.

On the subject of passion: another new position!
I place my left leg under your right, and my right
over it. This allows for maximum handplay.
Although, if the girl has sturdy thighs congress
can be difficult. We'll have to see, I hope.
Maybe the "Spinning Wheel" I mentioned is a bit
ambitious for us and we should try this one first?
Private B says when they did it his girlfriend sang
like a marsh toad. He grew up on a beetroot farm
and seems well informed on amphibians. Must go now
and scramble for firescraps as the company clowns
are again threatening to burn the remains of my boots.

Mrs Mop

When I asked my mam should I marry a soldier
she said if I loved him then I must.
We shared the richest cake my lips have touched
then he put on beret, black polished boots
and marched off into a November fog;
came back next spring, spoke of some damned
infernal place, the nearest to earthly hell.

When I heard of his posting I ran to the dock,
stood with young wives on the ferry's top deck
waving to one man lost in two thousand.
Back and forth we chugged the river,
all the fellers waving from the big ship
as we went on waving, always waving
into the long bitter winter night.

Moving On

In the far north the pines are gold and spicy
and stags guard hills of grey stone at dusk,
and swaying birches stand through the dark
like ghosts of peasants starved from their land.
Moving south, I stop at a pub and there's a feller
saying, "It looks like rain, you can sleep on my couch."
Striding back from Last Rock you walk
with spirits of ancient pagan folk, pass
granite altars and megaliths and mushroom quoits.
So we get to this feller's place and he starts
cooking for me, a big plate of pasta shells
and this sauce he learned from his aunt who used
to take him on the train to the beach but died
of the flu and still he misses her and remembers
how she'd take him on daytrips to the Tower.
In the High Peaks the space goes on for ever
as you stand on a rock like the head of a wild cat.
In the morning I can't get away, he keeps making tea
and wants me to see his collection of pebbles
and his little walled garden and the junk room
that gets the early sun and could be easily cleared.
The border lands are unpeopled mazes of larch
and spruce, tangles of holly and hawthorn and yew.
When I pick up my bag he says, "You can't go,
they might come; the thin one with the bony face
and the other one in the brown hat, you can't leave me alone."
I say, "Why don't you clear off out of it?"
He says, "They'd find me. They always do.
Last time they did my toenails, and I've got
nowhere to go. That's why you have to stay."
I say, "Haven't you got any friends?" He says, "You.
I'll put the kettle on shall I and make us a brew?"

Beat

New York, Denver, Frisco was the bohemian triangle,
and Beat is about feeling raw and cheated
and finding yourself a forest or a mountaintop,
and having sex in a lay-by, on a rooftop, down an alley.
And Neal Cassady couldn't stop, must always be moving,
and Lucien Carr's a wild kid up to capers and pranks,
and Wild Bill Cannastra would dance on broken glass.
Suddenly there's this clunking noise and a bang
and the back end drops and we're going nowhere,
watching the cars pass twenty miles from Knutsford.
You hung out in Greenwich Village dives
arguing Marx and Anarchy and Jean Paul Sartre
and saying one day you'd get real deep into Zen.
She says, "I told you to join the AA, now
I'll have to phone my mum to come and get us."
I said, "You can't do that, we're On The Road."
You pushed on right to the border and beyond,
a mattress and blankets in the back, milk and bread,
ciggies and whisky and weed; and talk, always talk
about Lincoln and Capone and the African Queen
and football and flowers and gossip and love;
you ease back and talk and empty yourself out
and move on down the freeway, always moving on.
She says, "Every car you've ever bought has been a dud,
those dealers must see you coming for miles."
Neal Cassady's heart gave out on whisky and pills
and Lew Welch disappeared to die in the woods
and Lucien Carr stabbed Dave Kammerer to death
and Cannastra was killed when he jumped from a train
and Kerouac went home to a mill town and his mum.

Without Trace

They made an example of Ronnie Kray for trying
to be an English Al Capone, and hooligan gangs
breed in vile byways said the Daily News in 1898,
and Henry the Fifth said, "Take no prisoners."
He married a king's daughter called Catherine,
which is a nice name, but my one was called Tracey.
So I said to her, "But it'll be my kid."
And she says, "What kind of father will you be,
coming and going, and mostly going. And you broke
into the Commo and stole the radiators."
I said, "That was last week, Trace, people change."
The Duke of Wellington was strong on tactics,
his cavalry smashed right through the French infantry.
I said, "I'm saying I'm gonna marry you, Trace,
I go the library now, and when have I ever hit you?"
She says, "Not yet, and I don't aim to give you the chance."
At Crecy the English bowmen cut the French to pieces
and Admiral Nelson said, "England expects every man
to do his duty." So he fell in love with a minister's wife.
Henry the Fifth and his missus lived in a palace.
I says to Tracey, "I told you what I wanted:
one of them new houses with the blue front doors
so I could artex your ceilings and creosote your fences.
I want to call my lad Buster and teach him to box."
She says, "My child will have the name I choose,
and my mam says you are a waster and a deadleg
without a civil thought in your head."
I says, "You what? You can't get more civil
than artexing someone's ceiling, can you?"
She says I'd get pissed and fall off the ladder.

Lager is a kind of light beer from Germany, also
a circle of armoured wagons. And at Rorke's Drift
a handful of Brits took on the Zulu army.
A lagger is a convict, and mafia means
hostility to law, and Marlon Brando hasn't
had to pay for a meal in an Italian restaurant
since he played the Godfather. I said, "Smile Trace,
the mob makes you offers you can't refuse, smile."
I said, "Admiral Nelson fell in love with Emma
and she had his kid; don't you see, he loved her.
Can't you understand what I'm saying, Trace? Trace?"

A Woman Of Letters

Scarlett O'Hara lost three husbands,
which like they say is very careless.
She rebuilds the family home
by making ball gowns out of curtains
but never appreciates Rhett Butler
and finishes up begging him to stay.
He says, "Frankly my dear I don't give a damn,"
and strides off into the sunset,
so you're left thinking tomorrow will be
another day, and wanting him to come back.
My feller likes Guinness. I keep a can
in the fridge, but he makes a cup of tea
when he gets here and then we go upstairs.
All happy families are happy in the same way
but unhappy families are unhappy
in their own way. Anna Karenina said that,
or Tolstoy. He's the one with the long beard
and a look on his face like he's just come home
and found his dinner in the dog's bowl.
Anna falls for Count Vronsky, under a train actually,
but that's at the end when he deserts her.
I put the condom in the glass ashtray
and then he slips it under his pillow.
The only problem with French letters is,
if you don't pay attention you get them inside out.
Madame Bovary's head is stuffed with romantic nonsense
but if you ask me Flaubert was one miserable bugger.
She gets married and thinks she's going to have
a wonderful time, which as we know is a big mistake.

Then she meets Rudolph, but he abandons her
when she wants to elope so she takes poison.
I make him chips and sometimes trifle
but I dyed my hair and he didn't even notice.
Then there's Clarissa who I believe takes
a hell of a long time to die, but life's too short
to read a book that thick. I said to him,
"Don't be surprised if I leap on top."
So I tried it and finished up quite dizzy.

The Meeting

Both our time charts were tight and blocked.
We met by arrangement and allowed fixed minutes
to contrast figures and graph lines,
to lay out plans for the next big thrust:
a season of waisted jackets and narrow bottoms.

It could have been the wine we shared
or it might have been what was meant to be;
our cases stood side by side, locks glaring
in a room of strange curtains and bedspread
as we unclothed ourselves in mid afternoon.

It was like being plucked from a prickly bush,
stretched far beyond your normal shape
and woven with smooth and unfamiliar strands;
like lengths of silk unrolling gently
down a very soft incline.